Favorite Classics
King Arthur
and the Knights of the Round Table

Retold by Sasha Morton
Illustrated by Alfredo Belli

An Hachette UK Company
www.hachette.co.uk

First published in the USA in 2013 by TickTock, an imprint of
Octopus Publishing Group Ltd
Endeavour House, 189 Shaftesbury Avenue, London WC2H 8JY
www.octopusbooks.co.uk
www.octopusbooksusa.com

Distributed in the US by Hachette Book Group USA
237 Park Avenue, New York NY 10017, USA

Distributed in Canada by Canadian Manda Group
165 Dufferin Street, Toronto, Ontario, Canada M6K 3H6

ISBN 978-1-84898-729-6

Printed and bound in China

10 9 8 7 6 5 4 3 2 1

With thanks to Lucy Cuthew

Contents

The Characters

Sir Ector

Uther Pendragon

Foster

Sir Kay

M

Arthur

Morgan le Fey

Guinevere

Mordred

Merlin

Sir Lancelot

Sir Galahad

Sir Bors

Sir Percival

Sir Bedivere

Chapter 1
The Legend of the Sword

Many years ago, there was a king called Uther Pendragon. He had fought many times against the Saxons, who wanted to steal his lands, and so he had many enemies.

When his son was born, he feared for the child's life, and so the king entrusted the baby to Merlin, a loyal friend and a man with magical powers. No one knew that the child even existed. When the king died, a stone holding a gleaming sword magically appeared in the churchyard. The sword bore a message:

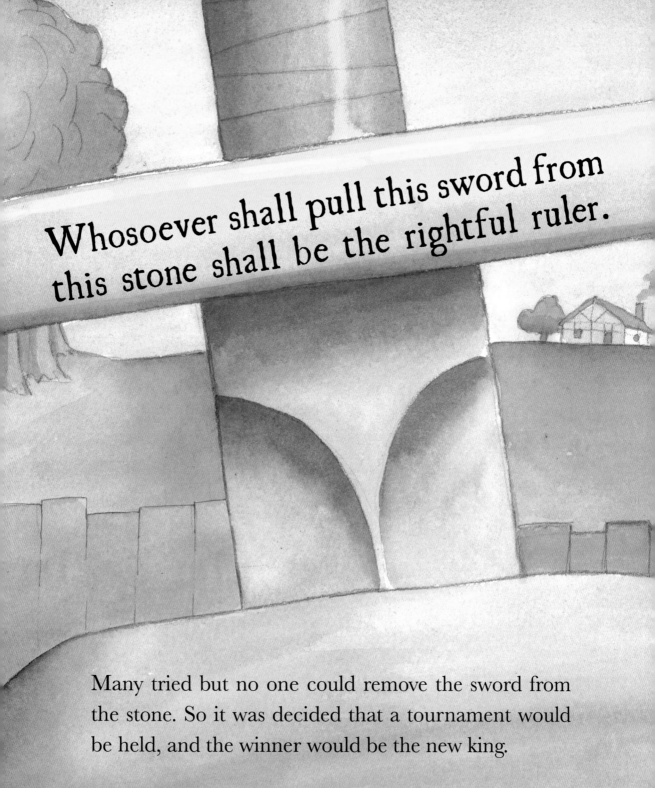

Whosoever shall pull this sword from this stone shall be the rightful ruler.

Many tried but no one could remove the sword from the stone. So it was decided that a tournament would be held, and the winner would be the new king.

A young lord named Sir Kay was taking part in the tournament, and his foster brother, Arthur, was looking after his weapons and armor.

Before Kay's first match, he called to his brother, **"Arthur, fetch me my lucky sword."**

To his shame, Arthur realized he had forgotten Kay's sword. Kay was furious. Suddenly, Arthur remembered the sword he'd seen sticking out of a rock on their way to the tournament. Maybe that would make a good replacement for Sir Kay?

He ran to fetch it.

8

Grabbing hold of the sword's handle, Arthur
pulled with all his might — and promptly fell **backwards!**
The sword slid easily from the stone.

Arthur hurried back to the tournament, but just before Sir Kay was about to take part in his match, his father saw the sword.

"Where did Kay's sword come from, Arthur?"
asked Sir Ector, with a frown.

"I found it sticking
out of a rock in
the churchyard. It was an odd place to leave such a
fine sword, but it was the first one I could find,"
explained Arthur.
Why did his father look so worried?

Sir Ector called together the people in charge of the tournament. Intrigued, they followed Arthur back to the churchyard. They placed the sword back into the stone, but no one could pull it free.

"It's easy," said Arthur. "You just pull it out like this!"

No one could believe that a young boy was able to do this when so many before him had failed.

This could only mean one thing...

Arthur was the rightful king!

Sir Ector explained that a magician named Merlin had asked him to take Arthur into his family sixteen years ago.

Until this day, they had no idea that the baby was Uther Pendragon's son.

Arthur was overwhelmed at what was happening to him.

To prepare him for becoming king, Arthur was knighted and a grand coronation ceremony was planned. But not everyone was convinced that a teenager should become king.

For Arthur, trouble was waiting just around the corner.

Chapter 2
Arthur the King

At Arthur's coronation, the crowd cheered and applauded the new **King of Britain.**

But there were some jealous dukes who didn't cheer, because they had wanted to rule themselves.

The most jealous of all was Uther Pendragon's daughter, Morgan le Fey.

She had assumed that one day she would become queen. And so while she smiled and pretended to welcome Arthur into her family, she began to secretly plot against him.

After the excitement of crowning the new king had died down, the British noblemen wanted to know just how Arthur intended to lead them.

Arthur went to Merlin. Arthur didn't always understand what Merlin was talking about, but Merlin was a friend and Arthur trusted him completely.

"I don't know how to be a king!" said Arthur in despair.

"Fear not," smiled the wise magician. "Once everyone sees your courage, bravery, and skill with a sword, they will follow you."

Arthur was determined to be
considered a worthy king.

He had a great sense of duty
and was willing to learn.

So he trained hard with his
sword and learned the laws
of the land.

Merlin's belief in Arthur was proved right. The young king's reputation for being a fearless swordsman grew and spread. He fought the Saxons and led battles against enemies. He showed that he could win wars and protect his country.

But Arthur was too trusting. He didn't notice that Morgan le Fey spied on him day and night. She hoped that he would be killed on the battlefield, and tried casting deadly spells on him.

Still Arthur was a **strong** and **brave** leader.

Even Morgan's clever tricks couldn't defeat him, for now…

Chapter 3
The Round Table

Soon King Arthur fell in love with a woman, Lady Guinevere, and they got married. It was a happy occasion and they were deeply in love.

On their
wedding day, Lady
Guinevere's father presented
Arthur with a huge, round table
to help him rule over his kingdom.
The table was exactly what was
needed to organize all of the
brave, but argumentative,
knights of Camelot.

Because it was round, each knight would be equal. At last, everyone would get along, and Arthur would be able to rule over a peaceful court.

Sir Lancelot

Each chair set at King Arthur's Round Table magically bore the name of the knight who belonged there.

One day, an injured knight was healed by a young squire named Lancelot. When Lancelot's name appeared on one of the remaining chairs, Arthur knighted him with the words,

"Arise, Sir Lancelot!"

Before long, Sir Lancelot became a good friend to the king and one of his most trusted allies.

Now, only one chair remained empty. Arthur was waiting for a hero with the most pure heart to sit in it, for it was believed that this knight would one day succeed in finding a treasure called the **Holy Grail.**

With his court almost fully assembled, Arthur decided that it was time to overcome the Saxons – who were trying to invade Britain again – once and for all. And so the Knights of the Round Table took on this enemy in a series of twelve bloody battles.

"Charge!"

Finally, the Saxons were defeated. Although some of Arthur's brave knights were lost, the nation was saved.

Chapter 4
Excalibur

During this war, Arthur broke the sword that he had pulled from the enchanted stone. Fortunately, Merlin knew just where to find a replacement.

"Where are you taking me, Merlin?"
asked Arthur, as they headed through a dark
forest towards a misty-looking lake.

"Are we lost?"

"No, your majesty.
We are not lost. Look!" replied Merlin.

Arthur watched in
amazement as a magnificent
sword rose out of the water. It was
held by a woman in long, flowing white
robes, who Merlin called the Lady of the Lake.

Arthur took the sword, which was called Excalibur, from the Lady of the Lake and she drifted gently back under the water.

Merlin explained more about the magnificent weapon to Arthur.

"This powerful sword was made on the mystical Isle of Avalon. The scabbard is even more precious than the sword," said Merlin. "So long as you have the scabbard, not one drop of your blood can be spilled. If it is lost, you may be killed again."

Little did either of them know that Morgan le Fey had followed them and was listening to their every word.

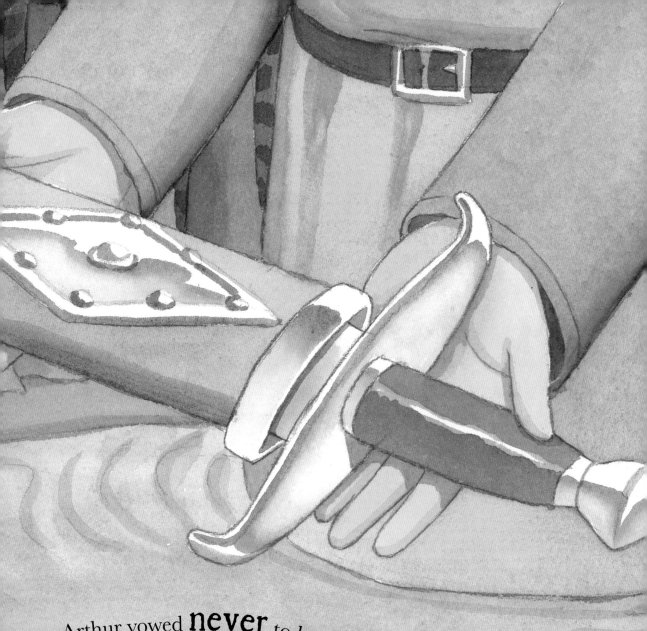

Arthur vowed **never** to let Excalibur out of his sight.

Yet from the shadows, Morgan vowed to do everything that she could to steal the precious scabbard away from Arthur.

Chapter 5

The Quest for the Holy Grail

A time of peace descended on Britain, but King Arthur's knights missed the thrill and adventure of battle.

"The knights need something heroic to do, Merlin. What do you suggest?"

Merlin smiled. "I will design some quests to keep them busy!"

Merlin was as good as his word.

Over the following years, he invented all sorts of interesting quests, from **hunting a white stag...**

30

But the good years passed, and bad times struck once more. People across the land were dying of starvation as their crops failed.

Merlin spoke to the knights of Camelot:

"It is said that the crops will grow again when a person with a pure heart finds the cup that was used by Jesus: the Holy Grail."

Sir Lancelot's son, Sir Galahad, was a brave, good, and pure young man. At Merlin's suggestion, Galahad sat in the last remaining seat at the Round Table.

After Sir Galahad took the seat, he had a vision of the Grail itself.

Immediately the king prepared his loyal knights for their most important quest.

Sir Galahad, Sir Percival, and Sir Bors decided to complete the Grail quest together, and set out bravely.

Soon they met Sir Percival's sister, who told them,

"You must follow me. Sir Galahad's grandfather, King Pelles, awaits you. He is the protector of the Holy Grail."

She led them to a ship that set sail across the sea to a distant shore. But not long after they landed, Sir Percival's sister died. Sir Bors took her body home and left Sir Galahad and Sir Percival to journey on to King Pelles' castle.

Arthur's knights travelled the land, searching for the Holy Grail. As many months passed, the number of knights returning to Camelot grew fewer and fewer.

Arthur despaired, especially as nothing was heard from brave Sir Galahad – his greatest hope.

When Sir Percival and Sir Galahad arrived at the castle of
King Pelles, they were led to his chamber. Sir Galahad
was saddened to see the elderly man was in great pain.

Just then two maidens entered the room, one with a spear, and one with a cup.

It was the Holy Grail!

Sir Galahad understood that he must take the spear and dip it in the cup and let a drop of blood from it fall onto King Pelles. He did so and the king was free of pain.

When they returned to their home, they found that at the same moment as Sir Galahad healed King Pelles, King Arthur's land had begun to bloom again. The crops grew and the famine was finally over.

Chapter 6
Mordred

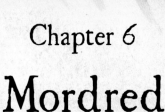

As the years
passed peacefully,
Morgan le Fey remained
desperate to take the throne
from Arthur. One night,
she finally succeeded in stealing
the magical scabbard from
King Arthur's sword.

Morgan le Fey no longer wanted the throne for herself,
but for her son, who was next in line to be king. Without the
scabbard for protection, she would be able to kill Arthur.

Now all Morgan and her evil son, Mordred, had to do was start a war...

Mordred went to Arthur and lied to him, saying that his wife, Guinevere, and Sir Lancelot were in love.

Heartbroken, Arthur had a dreadful argument with Queen Guinevere and she and Sir Lancelot fled across the sea to France for safety. Arthur left Mordred in charge of the country while he took the army to find the queen and Sir Lancelot.

While Arthur was in France, Mordred raised an army of his own. In fact, Mordred was so impatient to steal Arthur's throne, he decided to tell everyone that Arthur had been killed in battle in France. Without any delay, Mordred declared himself King of Britain!

RIP
King Arthur Killed in Battle

Long Live King Mordred!

Mordred assumed that without the magical scabbard
to protect him, Arthur would die in France.

He was mistaken.

The king heard of his
nephew's treachery and immediately
returned to England. But by the time
Arthur arrived back on England's
shores, a rebellion led by Mordred
was under way.

Mordred brought his entire army out to face King Arthur's men, and then there was a terrible battle. Soon, only a handful of soldiers were left on the battlefield. Arthur and Mordred came face to face.

"Nephew, you would have inherited my throne when I died. Let us stop this now," pleaded Arthur.

"Never!" roared Mordred.

With that, uncle and nephew fought to the death until finally, with one fatal slash of his sword, Arthur killed his enemy.

Exhausted, King Arthur *fell* to his knees.

He was the victor once more, but without Excalibur's magical scabbard, he knew he was close to death.

Chapter 7

The Death of Arthur

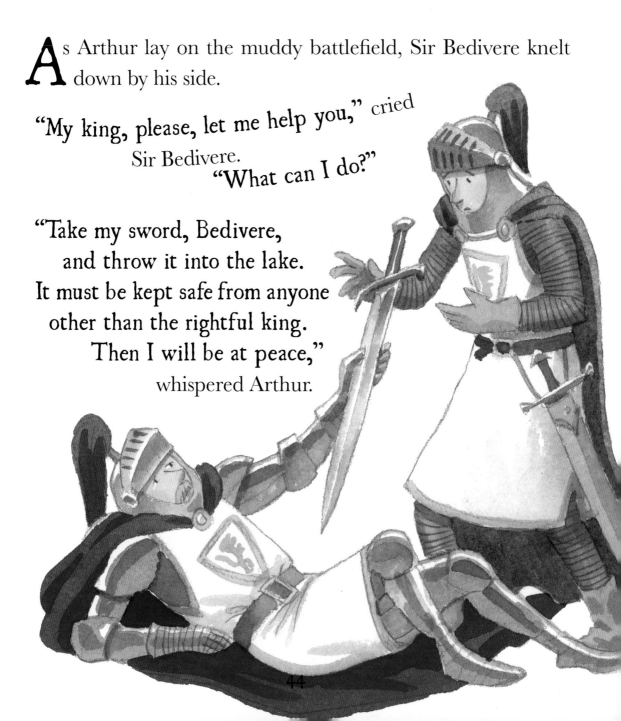

As Arthur lay on the muddy battlefield, Sir Bedivere knelt down by his side.

"My king, please, let me help you," cried Sir Bedivere. "What can I do?"

"Take my sword, Bedivere, and throw it into the lake. It must be kept safe from anyone other than the rightful king. Then I will be at peace," whispered Arthur.

Sir Bedivere nodded and took Excalibur from the dying king's hands.

When he arrived at the lake where Arthur had received Excalibur, Sir Bedivere hesitated. Surely Merlin would find some way to return the king to full health? If so, Arthur would need Excalibur back. So Sir Bedivere hid the magical sword under a bush and rode back to the battlefield as fast as his horse could gallop.

When Sir Bedivere reached the dying king, he realized that he had made the wrong decision.

"What happened when you threw Excalibur in the lake?" whispered Arthur.

"It sank, your highness," lied Sir Bedivere.

Arthur knew that if the knight had really returned the sword as he had asked, the Lady of the Lake would have taken it herself. He sent Sir Bedivere back to the lake.

Sir Bedivere threw the sword into the lake with all of his strength. As it whirled and glittered in the air, a hand broke the misty surface of the water.

The Lady of the Lake caught the sword and within moments it was gone.

This time, when Sir Bedivere described what had happened, King Arthur smiled and closed his eyes for the very last time.

Sir Bedivere stayed by Arthur's side until nightfall. As the sky darkened, three richly dressed women appeared at Arthur's side.

Silently, they lifted the king and took him to the water's edge, where a barge awaited. It was to take them to the mystical Isle of Avalon, where King Arthur Pendragon would forever be at peace.

When the sun rose the next day, it rose on a land without a king.

But it rose on a land that had created a legend.